# lulu's Chinese home food

# 中 式 家 常 菜

世界图书出版公司

上海·西安·北京·广州

# 前　言

　　笔者曾在英国留学多年，发现很多英国友人非常喜欢吃中国菜，并多次碰到有朋友向我索要中国菜谱以及问起怎样才能烧出地道的中国菜。在他们印象中制作中国菜是程序复杂、非常耗时、材料又很难买到的。对此我感到非常的诧异，并特地去了当地的书店及图书馆做了调查，结果却令我大吃一惊，只有一两本可以算得上是比较地道的中国菜谱，但也是十几年前出版的，其余都是西式中国菜或东南亚菜的混合菜式。为此我有了一个强烈的想法：出一本简单易学的中国家常菜菜谱，让更多的外国友人了解中国的饮食文化。

　　我的祖父上世纪 40 年代时曾在沪上开有两家传统饭店"六味斋"和"老公兴"。家里人都烧的一手好菜，因此我自小就耳濡目染地学会了很多传统中国菜的烧法和窍门。

　　通过一段时间的努力和尝试，我终于完成此菜谱。为了适合西方的读者，此菜谱的原料都经过精心挑选，选用的原料大部分都能在超市或中国城买到。

　　希望您看了本书后能改变您对烹饪中国菜的看法。如您能按照书上写的每道程序做的话，我能保证这会给您带来许多烹饪的乐趣，同时也可以品尝到地道的中国菜。

　　特此答谢在制作此书过程中向我提供很多帮助的好友David Whitsed，董辛冈，葛立新。竭诚希望读者多提宝贵意见，lululiu777@hotmail.com。

刘 陆 陆

2006 年 7 月

# Foreword

I spent several years living in England and found English people really like Chinese food. I was asked by different people many times how to recreate traditional Chinese home food. From this I decided to go to the library and book shop to find how many authentic Chinese recipe books there were. The result gave me a big surprise; only a few original Chinese recipe books exit. Some of them contain an Asian mix. I have a very strong desire to write one genuine Chinese recipe book and let people know true Chinese food.

Before people know Chinese food is very complicated to make and have no idea to find the ingredients. This book will totally change your mind. The cooking ingredients can easily be found in any Supermarket or China town. If you use correct way to cook, the process will be enjoyable.

My cooking inspiration and skill is from my family background. My grandfather was a chef, and owned two traditional restaurants, one called "Liu Wei Zhai" another is "Lao Gong Xing". When I was young, I always watched my grandparents and parents cooking. The good smell always attracted me. I tried to remember every process, so next time I would try by myself.

I would like to acknowledge my good friend David Whitsed, Xin gang Dong, Li xin Ge who gave me lots of help.

Finally, it remains for me to say I hope this book can broaden you cooking horizons and be useful to you. Any advice and opinion is welcome, please feel free to let me know, You can contact: lululiu777@hotmail.com. Enjoy!

Lu lu Liu
July 2006

lulu's Chinese home food

# Contents
# 目 录

Vegetable    8
蔬 菜

Meat    36
肉 类

Seafood    88
海 鲜

Rice Nood Desert    112
米饭、面食、甜品

Vegetable
蔬 菜

# 1. Cucumber salad

Preparation time 7 minutes

Ingredients: 1 cucumber

garlic, dried red chilli, sesame oil, vinegar, sugar, sea salt

Method:

1. Wash and dice the cucumber.
2. Place in a bowl, add a pinch of sea salt, a pinch sugar, a splash of vinegar and marinate for 5 minutes.
3. Remove the marinade and mix with 2 crushed garlic, 1 chopped dried red chilli and a touch of sesame oil and blend well.

This is a great way to liven up an ordinary cucumber.

## 凉拌黄瓜

准备时间7分钟

材　　料：1根黄瓜，蒜头，干红辣椒，芝麻油，醋，糖，海盐

做　　法：1. 洗净黄瓜然后切块。
2. 放入碗内，加一点海盐、糖，倒入醋腌制5分钟。
3. 加入2个拍碎的蒜头、1个切碎的干红辣椒和芝麻油，拌匀即可。

# 2. White radish salad

Preparation time 1 hour

Ingredients:    1/2 head of white radish

                      spring onion, sunflower oil, salt, sugar

Method:

1. Peel and slice the radish into halves and cut into long pieces.
2. Place the radish in a big bowl or a basin, drizzle 1/2 tablespoon of salt and blend well, cover with cling film and put in the fridge to marinate for 1 hour.
3. Make a dressing. Shredded the spring onions and place in a dish, add 3 tablespoons of oil and 1 teaspoon sugar and microwave for 30 seconds.
4. Take the marinated radish and drain any excess liquid.
5. Sprinkle the spring onions mix oil and sugar. Blend well and prepare to serve.

💡 This summer recipe is very traditional and gives great flavors.

## 凉拌萝卜

准备时间 1 小时

材　　料：半棵白萝卜，青葱，葵花油，盐，糖

做　　法：1. 把去皮后的萝卜，切成细长条状。
        2. 把切好的萝卜放在一个大碗或大盆内，撒上 1/2 汤匙的盐拌匀。盖上保鲜膜，放入冰箱腌 1 小时。
        3. 制作调料。把青葱切成小颗粒放入碗内，加入 3 汤匙油和 1 茶匙糖后放入微波炉里加热 30 秒。
        4. 拿出萝卜，沥干多余的水分。
        5. 加入制作好的调料，拌匀即可。

# 3. Aubergine salad

Preparation time 5 minutes + Cooking time 10 minutes

Ingredients:　　3 aubergines

　　　　　　　　chilli oil, sugar, sesame oil, garlic, soy sauce, salt

Method:

1. Cut the aubergine into two parts and put into steamer steam for 10 minutes until it becomes soft.
2. Prepare a sauce of 1 tablespoons of sesame oil, a pinch of salt, 2 drops of chilli oil, a teaspoon of soy sauce and 1/2 teaspoon of sugar.
3. Separate the aubergines into strips and pour over the sauce blend well.

In China aubergine is widely believed to reduce cholesterol. This is a filling side dish or accompaniment to a meal.

## 凉拌茄子

准备时间5分钟 + 烹饪时间10分钟

材　　料：3根茄子，辣椒油，糖，芝麻油，蒜头，酱油，盐

做　　法：1. 把茄子分成两段放入蒸锅内，蒸10分钟直至变软。
　　　　　2. 准备调料：1汤匙芝麻油、一撮盐、2滴辣椒油、1茶匙酱油和1/2茶匙糖。
　　　　　3. 把茄子分成长条，倒入调料拌匀即可。

# 4. Potato salad

Preparation time 12 minutes

Ingredients:     2 potatoes, 1/4 shallot, 3 pieces ham

                    mayonnaise, sugar

Method:

1. Heat the potatoes in the microwave for 10 minutes.
2. Peel off the skin then crush with the back of a spoon to a chunky pulp.
3. Shred a quarter of a shallot (can use a food proccessor) and 3 pieces of ham.
4. Mix the potato, shallot and ham with 1/2 teaspoon of sugar and 2 tablespoons of mayonnaise and blend well.

This salad suits a lunchbox or breakfast. The aroma of the shallots is wonderful and gives an edge to this simple recipe.

## 土豆色拉

准备时间 12 分钟

材　　料：2 个土豆，1/4 只红洋葱，3 片方腿，蛋黄酱，糖

做　　法：1. 土豆在微波炉中加热 10 分钟。

        2. 土豆去皮后用汤匙背压平成土豆泥。

        3. 把洋葱和 3 片方腿切碎（可用食品加工机）。

        4. 混合土豆泥、洋葱和方腿粒，再加上 1/2 茶匙糖和 2 汤匙蛋黄酱，拌匀即可。

# 5. Ma-po tofu

Preparation time 5 minutes + Cooking time 2 minutes

Ingredients:    1 bean curd cake

spring onion, sunflower oil, chilli bean sauce, soy sauce, sugar, salt

Method:

1. Remove any excess liquid from the bean curd and dice into 4cm cubes.
2. Heat oil in a wok and add 1/2 tablespoon chilli bean sauce, 1 teaspoon soy sauce and stir-fry for 10 seconds.
3. Add the bean curd and pinch of salt and 1/2 teaspoon sugar and 2 table-spoons water stir-fry for 30 seconds.
4. Turn down the heat and stir-fry for another 30 seconds.
5. Move onto the dish and garnish with chopped spring onions and serve.

Tofu is great source of protein and omega 3 fatty acids. Done this way it tastes good too!

## 麻婆豆腐

准备时间 5 分钟 + 烹饪时间 2 分钟

材　　料：1 盒豆腐，青葱，葵花油，辣豆瓣酱，酱油，糖，盐

做　　法：1. 把豆腐从盒内取出，沥干水分，再把豆腐切成 4 厘米的小块。

2. 锅内热油加入 1/2 汤匙辣豆瓣酱，1 茶匙酱油翻炒 10 秒钟。

3. 加入豆腐和一撮盐和 1/2 茶匙糖和 2 汤匙水翻炒 30 秒。

4. 开小火，再翻炒 30 秒。

5. 放入盘中，撒上青葱即可。

# 6. Bok choy fry mushrooms

Preparation time 5 minutes + Cooking time 3 minutes

Ingredients:     3 bok choy, 10 mushrooms

vegetable stock (optional), sunflower oil, salt

Method:

1. Chop the bok choy into thirds.
2. Thickly slice the mushrooms.
3. Heat the oil in a wok to a high heat and add the mushrooms, bok choy and a pinch of salt.
4. Stir-fry for 30 seconds then reduce the heat and add the 1/3 teaspoon vegetable stock to cook for a further 2 minutes.

You can buy bok choy in many supermarkets, but you should know there are a variety of ways to cook bok choy, not just steaming.

## 青菜蘑菇

准备时间5分钟＋烹饪时间3分钟

材　　料：3棵青菜，10个蘑菇，蔬菜精（选用），葵花油，盐

做　　法：1. 把每棵青菜切成三段。

2. 蘑菇切成厚片。

3. 把锅里的油加热后，放入蘑菇和青菜，外加一撮盐。

4. 翻炒30秒后，降低油温放入1/3茶匙蔬菜精（选用），再煮上2分钟。

# 7. Tomato scrambled eggs

Preparation time 8 minutes + Cooking time 5 minutes

Ingredients:     4 tomatoes, 3 organic eggs

spring onion, sunflower oil, tomato puree, salt, sugar

Method:

1. Finely chop the spring onions.
2. Slice the tomatoes into quarters and fry for 1 minute with 1 tablespoon of tomato puree and 1 tablespoon oil then set aside.
3. Beat the eggs with a pinch of salt.
4. Heat oil in a frying pan till hot then add the eggs fry 10 seconds and add the tomatoes and spring onions, a pinch of salt and sugar.
5. Stir-fry until the eggs are cooked satisfactorily.

Such a simple recipe, there are many different versions around the world, but this Chinese style is one of the most colourful and appealing.

# 番茄炒蛋

准备时间 8 分钟 + 烹饪时间 5 分钟

材　　料：4 个番茄，3 个草鸡蛋，青葱，葵花油，番茄酱，盐，糖

做　　法：1. 把青葱切成小段。
2. 把每个番茄切成 4 瓣，锅内放入 1 汤匙番茄酱和 1 汤匙油，炒 1 分钟后放在一边备用。
3. 放一撮盐，把蛋液打匀。
4. 锅内热油后加入鸡蛋炒 10 秒，加入番茄和青葱，再放一点盐和糖。
5. 翻炒直到鸡蛋变熟。

# 8. Green pepper fried potato

Preparation time 8 minutes + Cooking time 2 minutes

Ingredients:     2 potatoes, 2 green peppers

sunflower oil, garlic, vinegar, salt

Method:

1.  Chip the potatoes, crush the 2 cloves garlic and strip the green peppers.
2.  Heat the oil in a wok and quick hot fry garlic, potatoes and geeen peppers together for 30 seconds, adding 2 drops of vinegar and 1/2 teaspoon salt.
3.  Turn down the heat and lid on for 1 minute.

💡 The potato can be firm or soft depending on your taste.


## 青椒土豆丝

准备时间8分钟＋烹饪时间2分钟

材　　料：2个土豆，2个青椒，葵花油，蒜头，醋，盐

做　　法：1. 土豆切丝，拍碎2个蒜头，把青椒切成长条。
2. 锅内热油，放入蒜末、土豆丝和青椒丝快炒30秒，加入2滴醋和1/2茶匙盐。
3. 关上火，盖上锅盖焖1分钟即可。

# 9. Stewed aubergine

Preparation time 5 minutes + Cooking time 10 minutes

Ingredients:     1 large aubergine, 50g pork mince (optional)
dried chilli pepper, garlic, soy sauce, salt, spring onion, sunflower oil, chicken stock (optional)

Method:

1. Cut the aubergine into long strips or big chunks, heat the oil in a wok, put in the aubergine and quick fry until soft then set aside.
2. Heat the wok again and pour in 2 tablespoons oil, add 2 shredded garlic, 2 dried chillis, 2 springs onions with pork mince and a bit of salt and fry until the flavours release.
3. Add the aubergine and fry for 2 minutes. Add 3 tablespoons soy sauce and mix with 1/2 tablespoon of water, 1 teaspoon sugar and stir-fry for a further 3 minutes.
4. Turn down the heat, put on the lid and stew for 5 minutes.
5. Turn off the fire and garnish with shredded spring onions to finish.

The aubergine takes on a dark hue and delicate texture. It goes very well with rice.

## 油焖茄子

准备时间 5 分钟 + 烹饪时间 10 分钟

材　　料：1 根茄子，50 克猪肉糜（选用），干辣椒，蒜头，酱油，盐，青葱，葵花油，鸡精（选用）

做　　法：1. 把茄子切成长条或大块，锅内热油，放入茄子快速翻炒直至变软，放置一边。
　　　　　2. 锅内加热 2 汤匙油，加入 2 个拍碎的蒜头、2 个干辣椒、2 根青葱、肉糜和一撮盐一起翻炒直至香味溢出。
　　　　　3. 加入茄子炒 2 分钟，加入 3 汤匙酱油、1/2 汤匙水、1 茶匙糖。一起翻炒 3 分钟。
　　　　　4. 调至小火，盖上锅盖焖 5 分钟。
　　　　　5. 熄火，撒入葱粒即可。

# 10. Steamed egg pudding

Preparation time 5 minutes + Cooking time 10 minutes

Ingredients:    2 eggs

spring onion, sesame oil (pork fat), salt

Method:

1. Beat the eggs in a large bowl and mix with 1/2 teaspoon of salt, 1 cup of water and finely shredded spring onions.
2. Place the bowl in a wok, fill the wok with a layer of water and put on the lid to steam for 10 minutes.
3. Add 1/2 teaspoon of sesame oil ( pork fat) and serve.

Sometimes called egg soup, this is a perfect accompaniment to meat and vegetable dishes. If you want to increase the taste try experimenting with added prawns or mushrooms.

## 蒸　蛋

准备时间 5 分钟 + 烹饪时间 10 分钟

材　　料：2 个鸡蛋，青葱，芝麻油（猪油），盐

做　　法：1. 把鸡蛋、1 杯水、1/2 茶匙盐放入一大碗内快速搅拌，撒入葱粒。

　　　　　2. 把大碗放入锅内，锅内加水，盖上锅盖蒸 10 分钟。

　　　　　3. 加入 1/2 茶匙芝麻油（猪油）即可。

# 11. Spicy Chinese leaves

Preparation time 8 minutes + Cooking time 6 minutes

Ingredients:  1/2 head of Chinese leaves,

vegetable oil, chilli sauce, wild pepper, vinegar, salt

Method:

1. Separate the Chinese leaves, wash and strip.
2. Using a dry pan add several wild pepper pieces and stir-fry until the flavor start to release, then set aside.
3. Fry the Chinese leaves in hot oil until soft then turn down the heat.
4. Add 1 teaspoon of chilli sauce, 2 teaspoons vinegar and add the several wild pepper and a pinch of salt.
5. Stir-fry for 3 minutes then serve.

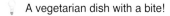 **A vegetarian dish with a bite!**

## 辣白菜

准备时间8分钟 + 烹饪时间6分钟

材　　料：半棵大白菜，蔬菜油，辣椒酱，花椒，醋，盐

做　　法：1. 把白菜掰开，洗净然后切成长条。

2. 在平底锅中加入花椒，翻炒直到香味溢出，放在一边备用。

3. 锅中倒入油加热。然后放入白菜翻炒，变软后调至小火。

4. 加入1茶匙辣椒酱、2茶匙醋、几粒花椒和一撮盐。

5. 再翻炒3分钟即可。

# 12. Spinach soup

Preparation time 2 minutes + Cooking time 8 minutes

Ingredients:  200g spinach, sweet corn, egg white,
vegetable oil, salt

Method:

1. Use a pot and pour 2 bowls of water and add 1 teaspoon of oil, 2 table-spoons of sweet corn and a pinch of salt  and heat until the water begins to boil.
2. Add the spinach (don't put the lid on) until it cooked.
3. Turn off the fire and pour in the egg white and blend well.

💡 This is fantastically healthy and very easy to prepare.

## 菠菜汤

准备时间2分钟＋烹饪时间8分钟

材　　料：200克菠菜，玉米粒，蛋清，蔬菜油，盐

做　　法：1. 在锅中倒入2碗水，再放入1茶匙油、2汤匙玉米粒和一点盐，加热直到水沸。
　　　　　2. 放入菠菜（不要加盖）直到煮熟。
　　　　　3. 关火，汤里浇入蛋清搅拌即可。

# 13. Vermicelli with fried tofu soup

Preparation time 10 minutes + Cooking time 5 minutes

Ingredients:     50g vermicelli, 3 fried tofu

spring onion, chicken soup, salt, sesame oil, chilli oil

Method:

1. Soak the vermicelli in hot water until completely soft.
2. Separate the fried tofu, heat 2 bowls of chicken soup in a pot until boil, add the vermicelli, fried tofu and 1/2 teaspoon salt then boil for a further 2 minutes.
3. Turn off the heat and drizzle 3 drops sesame oil and 2 drops chilli oil.
4. Sprinkle with finely chopped spring onions and serve hot.

This is a very traditional Shanghai soup.

## 油豆腐粉丝汤

准备时间 10 分钟 + 烹饪时间 5 分钟

材    料：50 克粉丝，3 个油豆腐，青葱，鸡汤，盐，芝麻油，辣椒油

做    法：1. 粉丝浸泡在热水中直至完全变软。

2. 掰开油豆腐，在锅内加热两碗鸡汤直到煮沸，加入粉丝、油豆腐、1/2 茶匙盐，再煮 2 分钟。

3. 关火，滴入 3 滴芝麻油和 2 滴辣椒油。

4. 撒入葱粒，热食。

Meat

肉 类

# 14. Celery with dried tofu and pork mince

Preparation time 10 minutes + Cooking time 6 minutes

Ingredients:     1 bunch of celery, 1 packet dried tofu, and 50g pork mince,
1/3 carrot
rice wine, sunflower oil, salt

Method:

1. Fry the pork mince in medium heated oil with rice wine and a little salt until cooked, then set aside.
2. Cut the dried tofu into strips and break the celery into chunky chips. Peel any excess woody strands from the celery, slice the carrot.
3. Reheat the wok with oil until the oil starts to evaporate, then add the celery, tofu, 1/2 teaspoon of salt, carrot and the pork mince.
4. Quick fry for 2 minute, then fry with the lid on for a further 1 minutes before serving.

Celery is a good food that is said to help people decrease their blood pressure. A special combination of flavours and textures makes this a favourite at dinner time.

## 芹菜豆腐干肉丝

准备时间 10 分钟 + 烹饪时间 6 分钟

材　　料：1 棵芹菜，1 包豆腐干，50 克猪肉糜，1/3 根胡萝卜，米酒，葵花油，盐

做　　法：1. 猪肉糜加入一点盐和米酒以中等油温炒熟，放一边备用。
2. 把豆腐切成细长条，把芹菜茎丝去除，掰成长条状，胡萝卜切片。
3. 锅内热油后加入芹菜、豆腐、肉丝、胡萝卜片和 1/2 茶匙盐。
4. 快速翻炒 2 分钟，然后盖上锅盖焖 1 分钟即可装盘。

# 15. Pork kidneys with green chilli

Preparation time 20 minutes + Cooking time 7 minutes

Ingredients:    2 fresh pork kidneys, 1 green chilli
garlic, thick slices of ginger, spring onion, groundnut oil, soy
sauce, rice wine, sesame oil

Method:

1. Wash the kidneys, removing the white fat and innards.
2. Cut into chunky cubes and scour the surface with crossed diagonal lines.
3. Parboil in water with a splash of rice wine and the 2 slices of ginger for 5 minutes then rinse in cold water.
4. Finely chop the 3 cloves of garlic then slice the green chillis into strips and remove the seeds.
5. Heat the oil in a pan and stir-fry the green chillis, garlic and kidneys. Add a splash 1/2 tablespoon soy sauce and pinch of salt to season.
6. Transfer to a plate and drizzle over some sesame oil and garnish shredded spring onions to serve.

💡 Pork kidneys contain rich proteins and minerals. Moreover, this is an excellent dish with a great blend of flavours.


## 青椒腰花

准备时间 20 分钟 + 烹饪时间 7 分钟

材    料：2 份猪腰，1 个绿色尖辣椒，蒜头，生姜，青葱，花生油，酱油，米酒，
芝麻油

做    法：1. 清洗猪腰，去除白色的内肠。
2. 切成块状，表面切成斜刀块。
3. 把猪腰放入一盛水的锅内，撒上米酒，放入 2 片姜片煮 5 分钟，然后用冷水洗净。
4. 把 3 个蒜头切碎，辣椒去籽切成长条。
5. 锅内热油翻炒辣椒，蒜末和猪腰。加入 1/2 汤匙的酱油和一撮盐。
6. 盛入盘中撒上切碎的青葱，淋上芝麻油。

# 16. Beef and radish stew

Preparation time 10 minutes + Cooking time 1 hour

Ingredients: 600g beef (beef shin), 1/2 white radish

spring onion, wild pepper, rice wine, sunflower oil, soy sauce, salt, fennel

Method:

1. Dice the beef into chunks of about 4-5cm.
2. Peel the radish and cut into triangular chunks.
3. Boil the beef in 2 bowls of water and add 1 tablespoon of wine until the water begins to run.
4. Drain the beef and wash with cold water.
5. Heat the oil in a wok and add fry the beef with several wild peppers, the fennels and pinch of salt until beef is light brown.
6. Transfer to a pot and add the radish, 1/2 bowl of water, 4 tablespoons soy sauce and chopped spring onions then simmer for 1 hour.

A warming stew with a bite! white radish is delicacy in China and has a more mellow flavour than the English equivalent, more like a turnip. The radish is rich in vitamin C.

## 萝卜牛腩

准备时间 10 分钟 + 烹饪时间 1 小时

材　料：600 克牛肉（牛腱），半棵白萝卜，青葱，花椒，米酒，葵花油，酱油，盐，茴香

做　法：1. 把牛肉切成 4~5 厘米的大块。
2. 萝卜去皮切成三角状。
3. 牛肉放入 2 碗水和 1 汤匙酒煮沸。
4. 沥干牛肉，用冷水洗净。
5. 锅内热油，然后加入牛肉和少许花椒翻炒，放入一点盐和茴香，直到牛肉颜色变深。
6. 把牛肉放入锅内，加入萝卜、1/2 碗水、4 汤匙酱油和葱段再煨 1 小时。

# 17. Roast duck legs

Preparation time 1 hour 30 minutes + Cooking time 34 minutes

Ingredients: 2 duck legs

light soy sauce, rice wine, crystallized cane sugar, ground-nut oil

Method:

1. Marinate the duck legs in 1 tablespoon of wine and 6 tablespoons of soy sauce for 1 hours.

2. Gently heat 80g crystallized cane sugar with 1 tablespoon of oil and water until the sugar dissolves to become a liquid.

3. Brush the sugar solution over the surface of the legs and leave for a further 20 minutes.

4. Preheat the oven to 190 ℃ (375 ℉ )and bake for 17 minutes, then turn over and bake for a further 17 minutes.

💡 So indulgent, the crispy golden-red duck is extremely tender and succulent.

## 烤鸭腿

准备时间 1 小时 30 分钟 + 烹饪时间 34 分钟

材　　料：2 个鸭腿，生抽酱油，米酒，黄冰糖，花生油

做　　法：1. 鸭腿淋上 1 汤匙酒和 6 汤匙酱油腌上 1 小时。

2. 在锅内慢慢加热 80 克冰糖使其融化，并加入 1 汤匙油和水。

3. 把糖油刷在鸭腿的表面上等 20 分钟。

4. 烤箱预热至 190 摄氏度（华氏 375 度），放入鸭腿，两面各烤 17 分钟即可。

# 18.　Avocado with beef mince

Preparation time 15 minutes + Cooking time 3 minutes

Ingredients:　　2 large avocado, 80g beef mince

red chilli, salt, onion, soy sauce, sugar, starch, white pepper powder, sunflower oil

Method:

1. Marinate beef with 1 teaspoon soy sauce, 1/2 teaspoon starch, 2 drops oil and a little white pepper powder. Blend well and leave for 8 minutes.
2. Split the avocado into halves and remove the stone. Place the fruit on a plate within the soft shell which will be used later.
3. Shredded red chillis and onions.
4. Heat the oil in the wok; add shredded onions, red chillis and the beef to fry for 1 minute. Sprinkle a little wine , add 1/2 teaspoon sugar, 1 teaspoon soy sauce, 1/2 teaspoon salt and the avocado then fry together for a further 2 minutes.
5. Spoon portions into the avocado's shell to serve.

The avocado must be very fresh, and put together with beef represents the classic yin and yang of Chinese cooking.

## 牛油果牛肉糜

准备时间 15 分钟 + 烹饪时间 3 分钟

材　　料：2个大牛油果，80克牛肉糜，红辣椒，盐，洋葱，酱油，糖，淀粉，白胡椒粉，葵花油

做　　法：1. 牛肉糜加1茶匙酱油、1/2茶匙淀粉、2滴油和少许白胡椒粉搅拌后等8分钟。
　　　　　2. 切开牛油果拿出果核，刮出果肉放入盘中，果壳备用。
　　　　　3. 把红辣椒及洋葱切碎。
　　　　　4. 锅内热油，加入洋葱粒、红辣椒和牛肉糜炒1分钟。淋入少许酒和1/2茶匙糖、1茶匙酱油、1/2茶匙盐和牛油果肉一块翻炒2分钟。
　　　　　5. 盛出果肉和牛肉糜放置在果壳内即可。

# 19. Beef and potato curry

Preparation time 15 minutes + Cooking time 30 minutes

Ingredients:　　300g diced chunks of beef, 1-2 potato

onion, curry powder, rice wine, groundnut oil, salt

Method:

1. Boil the beef in a pot with a bit of rice wine for few minutes until the water boils, then discard the water and wash the beef in cold water.
2. Heat some oil in a pan, add the curry powder and cook until the smell evaporates.
3. Chop the potatoes into chunks and chop 1 onion. Add to the pan with the beef and fry together.
4. Fry on a low heat with the lid on for a further 30 minutes.

💡 This is a brilliant curry dish popular in the South East Asia.

## 咖喱土豆牛肉

准备时间 15 分钟 + 烹饪时间 30 分钟

材　　料：300 克牛肉块，1~2 个土豆，洋葱，咖喱粉，米酒，花生油，盐

做　　法：1. 牛肉放入水中，加入少许米酒煮沸，倒去水再用冷水洗净。

2. 锅内放油加入咖喱粉，炒到香味溢出。
3. 土豆切成大块，1 个洋葱切碎与牛肉一起翻炒。
4. 盖上锅盖，用小火煮 30 分钟即可。

# 20. Spring onion chicken

Preparation time 30 minutes + Cooking time 2 hour 30 minutes

Ingredients:    1/2 chicken

water, rice wine, salt, soy sauce, Chinese five spices powder, fennel, spring onion, ginger, groundnut oil, coriander

Method:

1. Wash the chicken then put in a pot and add water to cover the chicken.
2. Add 1 tablespoon of wine, 1 tablespoon salt, 4 tablespoons soy sauce, 1/2 tablespoon five spices powder, 2 fennels.
3. Cover with a lid to boil for 10 minutes then turn down the heat and cook for 15 minutes before leaving to cool.
4. Leave the lid on for 2 hours then take out the chicken and drain. Move to a chopping board use a cleaver to cut into big chunks.
5. Display on a tray and sprinkle some shredded spring onions and ginger and 2 tablespoons of hot oil.
6. Garnish with several coriander leaves.

A tender chicken dish with a multitude of flavors to get the taste buds watering.


## 葱油鸡

准备时间30分钟 + 烹饪时间2小时30分钟

材　　料：半只鸡，水，米酒，盐，酱油，五香粉，茴香，青葱，姜片，花生油，香菜

做　　法：1. 把鸡洗净放入容器内，倒入水，水面盖过鸡。
　　　　　2. 加入1汤匙酒、1汤匙盐、4汤匙酱油、1/2汤匙五香粉、2个茴香。
　　　　　3. 盖上锅盖煮10分钟，然后开小火再煮15分钟，关火。
　　　　　4. 盖上锅盖焖2小时，待鸡冷却后拿出沥干。放到斩板上切块。
　　　　　5. 把切好的鸡放入盘中，撒上葱粒、姜末，淋上2汤匙热油。
　　　　　6. 用香菜装饰。

# 21. Beef stew tomatoes

Preparation time 30 minutes + Cooking time 1 hour 30 minutes

Ingredients: 300g chunk beef, 3 tomatoes

spring onion, ginger, rice wine, salt, soy sauce, tomato puree, chicken soup, sunflower oil, coriander

Method:

1. Chop the beef into big cubes then put in a pot with 1/2 tablespoon wine and enough water to cover the beef. Heat for a few minutes until water boils then discard the water and wash the beef.

2. Cut the 3 spring onions into 5cm long strips and slice the ginger into 3 pieces.

3. Heat the oil in a wok, first add the spring onions and ginger and stir-fry until the flavor releases.

4. Add the beef to quick fry for 1 minute then add 1/2 teaspoon salt, 2 tablespoons soy sauce and 300g chicken soup. First use high heat to cook until boiling then turn down the heat to simmer for 1 hour.

5. Add the chopped tomatoes and 100g tomato puree then further stew for 20 minutes.

6. Turn off the heat, move to a dish and garnish with coriander.

💡 A soup full of flavor and common as a starter in most Chinese restaurants, this dish is often overcooked, but can be regarded as a supplement to a main course.

## 番茄炖牛肉

准备时间30分钟 + 烹饪时间1小时30分钟

材　料：300克牛肉，3个番茄，青葱，姜片，米酒，盐，酱油，番茄酱，鸡汤，葵花油，香菜

做　法：1. 把牛肉切成大块放入锅内，加入1/2汤匙米酒和足够的水。加热直到水沸，然后倒掉水洗净牛肉。

2. 把3根青葱切成5厘米长的小段，然后把姜切成3片。

3. 锅内热油，先加入青葱和姜片翻炒直到香味溢出。

4. 加入牛肉快炒1分钟，然后加入1/2茶匙的盐，2汤匙酱油和300克鸡汤。先用大火煮直到煮沸，然后用小火炖1小时。

5. 加入番茄和100克番茄酱再煮20分钟。

6. 关火，装盘用香菜装饰，热食。

# 22. Hui guo pork

Preparation time 15 minutes + Cooking time 5 minutes

Ingredients:  300g pork with skin

spring onion, garlic, rice wine, soy sauce, salt, chilli bean sauce, sunflower oil

Method:

1. Wash the pork and put in a pot. Pour water over the pork and add 1 teaspoon rice wine to boil for a few minutes until the pork is cooked.
2. Drain the pork and slice into very thin pieces. Cut the spring onion to 4cm long strips and shred the garlic.
3. Heat the oil in a pan until the temperature is medium hot, add the pork and garlic to quick fry until the pork gains a little volume, then add 1 tablespoon chilli bean sauce and 1 teaspoon soy sauce and bit salt, stir-fry for 1 minute.
4. Add the spring onions and turn off the fire to serve.

This pork goes well with rice and vegetables.

## 回锅肉

准备时间 15 分钟 + 烹饪时间 5 分钟

材　　料：300 克猪肉带皮，青葱，蒜头，米酒，辣豆瓣酱，葵花油

做　　法：1. 清洗猪肉，放入一个锅内，倒入水盖过猪肉另外加 1 茶匙酒，煮几分钟直至猪肉煮熟。
2. 沥干猪肉，切成薄片，青葱切成 4 厘米长段，蒜头拍碎。
3. 锅内热油直至中度油温，加入猪肉和蒜末快速翻炒直至肉片翻卷。放入 1 汤匙辣椒酱、1 茶匙酱油、少许盐再翻炒 1 分钟。
4. 放入葱段，关火。

# 23. Curried chicken legs

Preparation time 10 minutes + Cooking time 5 minutes

Ingredients:　　5 chicken legs

onion, garlic, curry powder, rice wine, tomato puree, salt, sunflower oil

Method:

1. Put the chicken legs on a plate and sprinkle a bit of salt. Wait a few minutes then move to a steamer. Steam until completely cooked and turn off the heat.

2. Heat the oil in a wok and add the shredded onions and garlic, 2 teaspoons curry powder, 1/2 teaspoon wine and 1 teaspoon tomato puree. Mix and stir-fry then add the chicken legs to fry for 3 minutes.

3. Move the chicken legs to a plate and serve hot.

💡 **Extremely tasty and easy to prepare this takes no time at all**

## 咖喱鸡腿

准备时间 10 分钟 + 烹饪时间 5 分钟

材　　料：5 个鸡腿，洋葱，蒜头，咖喱粉，米酒，番茄酱，盐，葵花油

做　　法：1. 把鸡腿放在盘中撒上一些盐，等几分钟后移入蒸锅。蒸熟后关火。

2. 烧热油后加入切碎的洋葱和蒜末、2 茶匙咖喱粉、1/2 茶匙米酒和 1 茶匙番茄酱，翻炒，再加入鸡腿炒 3 分钟。

3. 把鸡腿移至盘内，热食。

# 24. Gong bao chicken

Preparation time 20 minutes + Cooking time 10 minutes

Ingredients:     300g chicken breasts, 100g peanuts
                 dried red chilli, wild pepper, soy sauce, vinegar, sugar, rice
                 wine, salt, ginger, garlic

Method:

1. Cut the chicken into small cubes and move to a small bowl then add 1 teaspoon soy sauce, 1/2 teaspoon salt, 1/2 rice wine, 2 pieces ginger, 1 egg white blend well and marinate for 10 minutes.

2. Put the peanut in a bowl of hot water to soak for a few minutes to allow the skin to separate and chop the 2 dried red chillis into tiny pieces.

3. Heat the oil in a wok then fry the peanuts until brown then remove to a tray.

4. Use the rest of the oil with dried red chillis, 2 shredded garlic cloves and several wild pepper pieces to fry until the flavors release. Add the chicken, quick fry for 3 minutes then add 1/2 tablespoon soy sauce, 1/2 teaspoon sugar, 2 drops vinegar and the peanuts to quick fry for a further 2 minutes.

This is a traditional dish of western China and really has a bite!

## 宫爆鸡丁

准备时间 20 分钟 + 烹饪时间 10 分钟

材　　料：300 克鸡胸脯肉，100 克花生，干辣椒，花椒，酱油，醋，糖，米酒，盐，姜片，蒜头，

做　　法：1. 把鸡肉切成鸡丁，放入一小碗内加入 1 茶匙酱油、1/2 茶匙盐、1/2 茶匙米酒、2 片生姜、1 个蛋清拌匀后腌 10 分钟。

　　　　　2. 把花生仁放入一个碗内，热水浸泡直至外层脱落，把 2 个干辣椒切成小丁。

　　　　　3. 锅内热油，翻炒花生直至颜色变深，放入另外一个盘内。

　　　　　4. 用剩余的油炒干辣椒、2 个蒜头末和花椒，直至香味溢出时加入鸡丁。快速翻炒 3 分钟加入 1/2 汤匙酱油、1/2 茶匙糖、2 滴醋和花生一起炒 2 分钟。

# 25. Cha shao

Preparation time 5 hours + Cooking time 50 minutes

Ingredients:　　500g loin of pork (off the bone and skin removed)

　　　　　　　　cha shao jam, rice wine, honey

Method:

1. Marinate the pork with cha shao jam and 1 teaspoon wine on a plate, cover with cling film and move to the refrigerator to rest for 5 hours.
2. Using a preheated oven to 210℃, bake the pork for 40 minutes.
3. Take out the pork and drizzle over several spoons of honey and bake for a further 10 minutes.
4. Remove the pork from the oven and slice into thick pieces.

💡 The original spare rib recipe, it is so easy to make and is an excellent addition to a barbeque.

## 叉　烧

准备时间 5 小时 + 烹饪时间 50 分钟

材　　料：500 克猪里脊肉（去皮和骨），叉烧酱，米酒，蜂蜜

做　　法：1. 腌猪肉，在碗里加入 1 茶匙酒和叉烧酱盖上保鲜膜放入冰箱腌 5 小时。

　　　　　2. 烤箱温度 210 摄氏度，放入猪肉烤 40 分钟。

　　　　　3. 取出猪肉排淋上几匙蜂蜜再烘烤 10 分钟。

　　　　　4. 从烤箱内取出烤好的猪肉并切片。

# 26. Easy microwave chicken wings

Preparation time 1 hour + Cooking time 6 minutes

Ingredients:     6 chicken wings

spring onion, ginger, soy sauce, oyster sauce, sunflower oil, sugar, sesame oil

Method:

1. Marinate the wings in 5 tablespoons soy sauce and 1 teaspoon wine and put 3 slices of ginger for 1 hour.
2. Heat 1 tablespoon of oil on a plate in the microwave for 1 minute.
3. Add the marinated wings and microwave under cling film for 2 minutes.
4. Prepare a sauce containing 1 tablespoon of soy sauce, 1 teaspoon of sugar, 1 tablespoon oyster sauce, 1 teaspoon sesame oil and finely chopped spring onions.
5. Add the sauce to the wings, mix well then cover in cling film and microwave for a further 3 minutes.

This is a simple way of preparing a snack or an accompaniment to a feast.

## 微波炉鸡翅

准备时间1小时+烹饪时间6分钟

材　　料：6个鸡翅，青葱，姜片，酱油，蚝油，葵花油，糖，芝麻油

做　　法：1. 用5汤匙酱油，3片姜片和1茶匙酒腌制鸡翅1小时。
2. 把1汤匙油加入一个盘中，放入微波炉加热1分钟。
3. 放入腌好的鸡翅，盖上保鲜膜放入微波炉里加热2分钟。
4. 准备调料，1汤匙酱油、1茶匙糖、1汤匙蚝油、1茶匙芝麻油和切碎的青葱。
5. 把调料和鸡翅搅拌，盖上保鲜膜放入微波炉再加热3分钟即可。

# 27. Pork with eggs

Preparation time 10 minutes + Cooking time 30 minutes

Ingredients: 300g diced pork, 4 eggs

spring onion, ginger, ground nut oil, soy sauce, rice wine, sugar, salt

Method:

1. Hard boil the eggs for 10 minutes.
2. Place in cool water for a while and knock the egg remove the shell and slash 3 times on egg surface.
3. Fry the pork in oil and add 1 teaspoon of wine and a pinch of salt until brown.
4. Add the eggs and 5 tablespoons soy sauce, 1/2 teaspoon sugar, 2 pieces of ginger and 2 spring onions.
5. Cover and stew on a low heat for 1 hour.

This is another great dish. The pork compliments the egg and the taste is fantastic.

## 肉焖蛋

准备时间 10 分钟＋烹饪时间 30 分钟

材　　料：300 克猪肉，4 个鸡蛋，青葱，生姜，花生油，酱油，米酒，糖，盐

做　　法：1. 大火煮鸡蛋 10 分钟。

2. 把鸡蛋放入冷水中冷却，然后去壳，在每个鸡蛋上划三刀。
3. 炒猪肉然后加上 1 茶匙酒和一撮盐，然后炒熟。
4. 加入蛋、5 汤匙酱油、1/2 茶匙糖、2 片姜和 2 根青葱。
5. 盖上锅盖小火焖 1 小时。

## 28. Sichuan kou shui chicken

Preparation time 1 hour 40 minutes + Cooking time 30 minutes

Ingredients:　　1 small chicken

ginger, spring onion, sugar, dried red chilli, soy sauce, ginger oil, vinegar, sesame jam, chilli oil, garlic oil, wild pepper oil, peanuts

Method:

1. Tie the spring onions into knots with the chicken, and add 3 pieces of ginger, rice wine and salt  boil for 40 minutes.
2. Move the chicken from hot water, soak the chicken in cool water and move to refrigerator for 1 hour.
3. Prepare a sauce of 2 tablespoons of soy sauce, 2 dried chillis, 1 teaspoon ginger oil, 1 tablespoon of sesame jam, 1 teaspoon of chilli oil, 1 teaspoon wild pepper oil, 1 teaspoon garlic oil and a touch of vinegar and a pinch of sugar.
4. Fry the peanuts until brown.
5. Drain and cut the chicken into strips, pour over the sauce and garnish with the cooked peanuts and shredded spring onions.

💡 **This is spicy chicken to die for!**

## 四川口水鸡

准备时间 1 小时 40 分钟 + 烹饪时间 30 分钟

材　　料：1 只童子鸡，姜片，青葱，糖，干辣椒，酱油，生姜油，醋，芝麻酱，辣椒油，大蒜油，花椒油，花生

做　　法：1. 鸡放入锅内，倒入水，放入 1 个葱结，3 片姜片，少许米酒和盐一起煮 40 分钟。
2. 把鸡从热水里盛出，浸在冷水里，放入冰箱 1 小时。
3. 准备调料，2 汤匙酱油、2 个干辣椒、1 茶匙生姜油、1 汤匙芝麻酱、1 茶匙辣椒油、1 茶匙花椒油、1 茶匙大蒜油、少许醋和糖。
4. 把花生炒熟。
5. 把鸡沥干并切成长条，倒入调料，并用花生和葱粒装饰。

# 29. Pineapple beef

Preparation time 40 minutes + Cooking time 10 minutes

Ingredients:      400g beef, 250g pineapple

red pepper, green pepper, garlic, soy sauce, salt, sesame oil, white pepper powder, oyster sauce, groundnut oil

Method:

1. Peel the pineapple and cut into big chunks, dice the green pepper and red pepper.
2. Cut the beef into cubes and move to a tray. Add 1 tablespoon soy sauce, 1/2 teaspoon sesame oil, 1 teaspoon oyster sauce, 1/2 teaspoon sugar, drizzle bit white pepper powder and marinate for 30 minutes.
3. Heat oil in a hot pan, add the beef and fry both sides until cooked then move to a tray.
4. Use the remaining oil to quick fry 3 shredded garlic cloves until the flavor releases, add the red pepper, green pepper and pineapple to quick fry for 1 minute then adding the beef stir-fry 2 minutes.

💡 This sweet and savory dish is a version of the well known sweet and sour dish.

## 菠萝牛肉

准备时间 40 分钟 + 烹饪时间 10 分钟

材　　料：400 克牛肉，250 克菠萝，红椒，青椒，蒜头，酱油，盐，芝麻油，白胡椒粉，蚝油，花生油

做　　法：1. 菠萝去皮切成大块，青椒和红椒切成小块。
2. 把牛肉切成块放入一个盘中，加 1 汤匙酱油、1/2 茶匙芝麻油、1 茶匙蚝油、1/2 茶匙糖，撒一点白胡椒粉腌 30 分钟。
3. 锅内热油，加入牛肉煎至两面均熟后移入盘内。
4. 用剩余的油快炒 3 个拍碎的蒜头直到香味溢出。加入红椒、青椒、菠萝快炒 1 分钟，加入牛肉再翻炒 2 分钟。

# 30. Cauliflower with pork

Preparation time 10 minutes + Cooking time 3 minutes

Ingredients:　　1 head of cauliflower, 200g sliced pork, 3 dried mushrooms (optional)

garlic, salt, starch, sunflower oil

Method:

1. Separate the cauliflower and with the dried mushrooms add to a pot, pour in water and boil until soft. Drain for later use.
2. Pat some starch flour on the sliced pork.
3. Heat the oil in a wok, add 3 shredded garlic and fry until it becomes brown then add the pork to further fry for 1 minute.
4. Mix the cauliflower and mushrooms with the pork and fry for 2 minutes with a pinch of salt.

This recipe is known for its excellent flavour. Especially if you enjoy the taste of garlic!

# 花菜肉片

准备时间 10 分钟 + 烹饪时间 3 分钟

材　　料：1 棵花菜，200 克猪肉片，3 个香菇（选用），蒜头，盐，淀粉，葵花油

做　　法：1. 掰开花菜，和香菇一起放入锅内加入水煮至变软，沥干备用。
2. 拍一些淀粉在猪肉片上。
3. 锅内热油，放入 3 个蒜头翻炒，直至颜色变成棕色后放入猪肉片再炒 1 分钟。
4. 放入花菜、香菇、一撮盐，和猪肉再炒 2 分钟即可。

# 31. Cheese pork steak

Preparation time 20 minutes + Cooking time 10 minutes
Ingredients:　　2 pork steak, 2 pieces of cheese
　　　　　　　　bread crumbs, egg white, salt, rice wine, white pepper powder, groundnut oil

Method:

1. Slice the steaks into two thinner pieces.
2. Use a hammer to flatten and tenderize both sides of the steaks, add a piece of cheese between two pieces of meat, press well together and move to a tray.
3. Sprinkle with salt and white pepper powder and little wine, leave for 10 minutes then brush with the egg white.
4. Pour the bread crumbs into a tray, add the pork steak and touch the flour on both sides so that it completely covers the meat.
5. Heat the 50g oil in a pan, use a medium heat to fry the pork until browned on both sides. Serve hot.

This dish has its roots in Chinese recipes, but with influence from the western recipes.

## 干酪猪排

准备时间 20 分钟 + 烹饪时间 10 分钟
材　　料：2 块猪排，2 片干酪，面包粉，蛋清，盐，米酒，白胡椒粉，花生油

做　　法：1. 把猪排切成两薄片。
　　　　　2. 用一小锤把猪排敲成薄片，在两片之间加入一片干酪，压紧放入盘内。
　　　　　3. 猪排两面撒上盐和白胡椒粉、一些米酒，等 10 分钟然后刷上蛋清。
　　　　　4. 在盘内放入面包粉，再放入猪排，两面沾上面包粉直至完全包裹。
　　　　　5. 锅内热 50 克油，用小火煎至猪排两面颜色变成金黄色，热食。

# 32. Snap peas with Chinese sausage

Preparation time 6 minutes + Cooking time 4 minutes

Ingredients:　　1 Chinese sausages, 400g snap peas

　　　　　　　　groundnut oil, salt

Method:

1. Cut off both ends of the snap peas.
2. Slice the sausages into thin shapes.
3. Fry the sausage in a hot wok for 1 minutes.
4. Add the peas and fry for a further 3 minutes with a pinch of salt.

**A great combination of vegetable and meat!**

## 荷兰豆炒香肠

准备时间6分钟+烹饪时间4分钟

材　　料：1根香肠，400克荷兰豆，花生油，盐

做　　法：1. 把荷兰豆的两端去除。

　　　　　2. 香肠切薄片。

　　　　　3. 把香肠用油煎1分钟。

　　　　　4. 加入荷兰豆和一撮盐，炒3分钟即可。

# 33. Fried beef strips with celery

Preparation time 10 minutes + Cooking time 3 minutes

Ingredients:     200g beef strips, 1 celery
                 soy sauce, starch, groundnut oil, rice wine, salt

Method:

1. Marinade the beef in 1 teaspoon starch and 2 teaspoons soy sauce and 1/2 teaspoon rice wine for 7 minutes.
2. Break the celery into chunky chips, peel any excess woody stands.
3. Stir-fry the beef in a hot wok for 1 minute then add 1/2 teaspoon salt and the celery fry for a further 2 minutes.

This is very easy and filling. The ingredients compliment each other well.

## 芹菜牛肉丝

准备时间 10 分钟 + 烹饪时间 3 分钟

材　　料：200 克牛肉丝，1 棵芹菜，淀粉，酱油，花生油，米酒，盐

做　　法：1. 用 2 茶匙酱油，1 茶匙淀粉和 1/2 茶匙米酒腌牛肉丝 7 分钟。
　　　　　2. 芹菜掰成长条状，把茎丝去除。
　　　　　3. 先翻炒牛肉 1 分钟，然后加入 1/2 茶匙盐加入芹菜，再翻炒 2 分钟。

# 34. Big meat ball

Preparation time 15 minutes + Cooking time 10 minutes
Ingredients:　　500g pork mince (beef mince), 2 water chestnuts (optional)
　　　　　　　　salt, rice wine, white pepper powder, spring onion, ginger,
　　　　　　　　starch, egg white, groundnut oil a: (soya sauce, sugar), b:
　　　　　　　　(chicken soup, egg yolk)

Method:

1. Mix pork mince with 2 crushed water chestnuts, 1 teaspoon wine, 1 teaspoon salt, a bit of shredded ginger and spring onions, white pepper powder, 1 egg white, a bit of starch and blend well until sticky.
2. Divide the pork mince into 2 portions, and hand form each into a ball.
3. a. You can use oil to fry until the meat balls become brown, then add 4 tablespoons soy sauce and a little sugar. The red stew meat balls combine well with cooked bok choy.
   b. You can put the meat balls in a big bowl; pour in 70g chicken soup and steam for 30 minutes. If you want meat balls to be more colourful, you can brush some egg yolk on the surface before steam.

This can be combined with cooked bok choi. The water chestnuts add a rare texture to the meatballs. You must try!

## 狮子头

准备时间 15 分钟 + 烹饪时间 10 分钟
材　　料：500 克猪肉糜（或牛肉糜），2 个荸荠（选用），盐，米酒，白胡椒粉，青葱，姜片，
　　　　　淀粉，蛋清，花生油　　方法一：酱油，糖　　方法二：鸡汤，蛋黄

做　　法：1. 猪肉糜和 2 个切碎后的荸荠一起搅拌，加入 1 茶匙米酒、1 茶匙盐、少许葱粒姜末和白胡椒粉、1 个蛋清、少许淀粉。搅拌均匀直到有黏稠感。
　　　　　2. 把猪肉糜分成 2 份，用手搓成球状。
　　　　　3. 方法一：可用油炸肉丸直至颜色变深。再放入 4 汤匙酱油和一点糖。红烧狮子头放些青菜做配饰。
　　　　　　方法二：可把肉丸放在大碗里，放入 70 克鸡汤蒸煮 30 分钟。如果想狮子头看上去颜色鲜艳些，可在蒸之前涂上点蛋黄。

# 35. Chicken fry bean sprouts

Preparation time 10 minutes + Cooking time 5 minutes

Ingredients:    300g chicken breast, 200g bean sprouts

salt, egg white, white pepper powder, sunflower oil

Method:

1. Cut the chicken breast into long strips, add 1/2 teaspoon of white pepper powder and 1 egg white, to marinate for 6 minutes.

2. Heat the oil in a wok and add chicken to quick fry until the chicken is half-cooked then add the bean sprouts, and 1/2 teaspoon salt together stir-fry a further 3 minutes.

Enjoy this simple dish with your own choice of spices!

## 银芽鸡丝

准备时间 10 分钟 + 烹饪时间 5 分钟

材    料：300 克鸡脯肉，200 克银芽，盐，蛋清，白胡椒粉，葵花油

做    法：1. 把鸡脯肉切成细长条，加入 1/2 茶匙白胡椒粉、1 个蛋清腌 6 分钟。

2. 锅内热油，加入鸡肉快速翻炒直到半熟加入银芽和 1/2 茶匙盐一起翻炒 3 分钟。

# 36. Bok choy meatball soup

Preparation time 8 minutes + Cooking time 10 minutes
Ingredients:     2 bok choy, 200g pork mince, 8 button mushrooms (optional)
spring onion, ginger, egg white, salt, vegetable oil

Method:

1. Make the meatballs with the pork mince add 1 teaspoon egg white, shredded ginger, shredded spring onion and a bit of salt.
2. Cut the bok choy into 3 parts and slice the mushrooms.
3. Heat the oil in a wok, fry the meatballs until they are lightly brown.
4. Heat a pot with 2 bowls of water and add the meatballs until boiling, then add the bok choy and mushrooms to boil together for 1 minute with a pinch of salt.

So healthy, so delicious!

## 青菜肉丸汤

准备时间 8 分钟 + 烹饪时间 10 分钟

材　　料：2 棵青菜，200 克猪肉糜，8 个小蘑菇（选用），青葱，生姜，蛋清，盐，蔬菜油

做　　法：1. 猪肉糜内放入 1 茶匙蛋清、一点姜末、葱粒和一撮盐，然后做成几个肉丸。
　　　　　2. 青菜切成 3 段，蘑菇切片。
　　　　　3. 锅内热油，把肉丸炸成金黄色。
　　　　　4. 锅内放入 2 碗水和肉丸加热直到煮沸，放入青菜和蘑菇，加点盐再煮 1 分钟。

# 37. Luo song soup

Preparation time 30 minutes + Cooking time 35 minutes

Ingredients:     200g diced beef, 4 tomatoes, 1 onion, 1/2 head of Chinese cabbage

sunflower oil, tomato puree, rice wine, salt, vinegar, white pepper powder, milk

Method:

1. Boil the beef in water and add a little wine until the water running and discarding the water and wash the beef use cold water then drain.

2. Slice the tomato into 4 pieces then stir-fry with 5 tablespoons tomato puree, a pinch of salt and sugar.

3. Chop the cabbage and onion and quick fry for a couple of minutes until the aroma of the ingredients begin to release.

4. Add the beef to the cabbage, onions and tomatos mix to a pot. Add 3 bowls of water and 1/2 teaspoon vinegar, 1 teaspoon salt and 2 tablespoons milk and boil for 30 minutes. Turn off the fire, drizzle a bit white pepper powder.

💡 Luo song soup can be equally brilliant with or without the beef.

## 罗宋汤

准备时间30分钟 + 烹饪时间35分钟

材　料：200克牛肉块，4个番茄，1个洋葱，1/2棵卷心菜，葵花油，番茄酱，米酒，盐，醋，白胡椒粉，牛奶

做　法：1. 牛肉放入水中煮加入一些酒，等到煮沸时用冷水洗后沥干。

2. 番茄切成4瓣入锅，加入5汤匙番茄酱，加入一点盐和糖，一起翻炒。

3. 卷心菜和洋葱切碎，放入锅内快速翻炒直至香味溢出。

4. 把3碗水倒入锅内，加入牛肉、卷心菜、洋葱和番茄。放入1/2茶匙醋、1茶匙盐和2汤匙牛奶，煮30分钟。关火后撒些白胡椒粉即可。

# 38. Hot pot

Preparation time 10 minutes + Cooking time 1 hour 30 minutes
Ingredients:     300g pork chop, 1/2 chicken
                 water, spring onion, garlic, salt, (dried red chilli, chilli oil)

Method:
1. Put the pork chop and 1/2 chicken in a big pot, add enough water to cover and 1 tablespoon of wine and salt. Heat until boiling then discard the water and add some new cool water. Heat until boiling again and simmer for 1 hour.
2. Add 2 knots of spring onion, 3 pieces of ginger, 3 cloves of garlic, and if preferred, dried chillis or chilli oil for more spice.
3. Prepare a range of raw meat, fish, seafood and vegetable pieces (whatever you like) to place in the hot pot until cooked.
4. Put together a range of dips for meat, fish and vegetables. For example: soy sauce, oyster sauce, sesame jam, chilli sauce, sesame oil, fish sauce or black pepper sauce, coriander.

This method of cooking is similar to the French fondu, where diners cook their own food in a boiling soup. It's great for cold winter nights or at a dinner party.

# 火 锅

准备时间 10 分钟 + 烹饪时间 1 小时 30 分钟
材　　料：300 克猪骨，半只鸡，水，青葱，蒜头，盐，（红辣椒，辣椒油）

做　　法：1. 把猪骨和半只鸡放入一大锅内。倒入足够的水、1 汤匙酒和盐，加热直至煮沸。把水倒掉，洗净。再倒入冷水煮开后再煨 1 小时。
　　　　　2. 放入 2 个葱结、3 片姜片、3 个蒜头。如果喜欢辣味，可以放几个干辣椒或少许辣椒油。
　　　　　3. 准备一些肉类、鱼、海鲜和蔬菜。任由你组合，放入锅内烫熟。
　　　　　4. 如需蘸料，可以自己制作一个调料。可选用：酱油，海鲜酱，芝麻酱，辣椒酱，芝麻油，鱼露，黑胡椒汁，香菜。

# Seafood

# 海鲜

# 39. King prawn stew

Preparation time 10 minutes + Cooking time 6 minutes

Ingredients:　　300g king prawns

spring onion, ginger, sugar, rice  wine, soy sauce, tomato paste, fish sauce, sunflower oil, salt

Method:

1. Wash the prawns and de-veined.
2. Marinate in 1 tablespoon of rice wine and a pinch of salt for 5 minutes.
3. Fry 2 tablespoons of sunflower oil with 1 tablespoon soy sauce, chopped spring onions and 2 slices of ginger.
4. Add the prawns and stir-fry until a pink colour comes through.
5. Add 1 teaspoon of tomato paste, 1 teaspoon of fish sauce, a pinch of salt, a pinch of sugar and cover stew for 1 minute.
6. Uncover then fry on a high heat for a further minute.
7. Sprinkle some chopped spring onions and serve.

Prawn have an abundance of nutritional value containing calcium, phosphor and iodine minerals with vitamin A. Cooked this way, the meat is very tender and easily digested.

## 油爆虾

准备时间 10 分钟 + 烹饪时间 6 分钟

材　　料：300 克大虾，青葱，姜片，糖，米酒，酱油，番茄酱，鱼露，葵花油，盐

做　　法：1. 把虾洗净，用刀去除背部黑线。

2. 用 1 汤匙米酒和少量盐腌 5 分钟。
3. 用 2 汤匙葵花油翻炒 2 片姜，少许葱粒和 1 汤匙酱油。
4. 加入大虾翻炒直到虾的颜色变成粉红色。
5. 加入 1 茶匙番茄酱、1 茶匙鱼露、少许盐和糖，盖上锅盖焖 1 分钟。
6. 开盖用大火炒几分钟。
7. 撒上葱粒即可。

# 40. Steamed eel

Preparation time 20 minutes + Cooking time 10 minutes

Ingredients:     1 eel

spring onion, ginger, salt, sugar, white pepper powder, rice wine, pork fat, sunflower oil

Method:

1. Gut the eel and use the hot water to scale the eel's skin.
2. Wash the eel and use the cleaver cut into thick pieces, and display in a circle on a flat tray.
3. Using a sauce pan add 1 teaspoon salt, 1/2 teaspoon sugar, 1/2 teaspoon white pepper powder, 1 teaspoon rice wine, a bit of pork fat then blend well and drizzle evenly on the eel.
4. Cover with cling film and place in the steamer. Use a high heat for 7 minutes then turn off the heat with lid on for a further minute.
5. Remove the film and garnish with shredded spring onions and ginger then drizzle over a little cooked sunflower oil.

A favorite, the eel is an excellent source of protein and retains a delicate texture and flavor cooked this way

## 蒸鳗鱼

准备时间 20 分钟 + 烹饪时间 10 分钟

材　　料：1 条鳗鱼，青葱，生姜，盐，糖，白胡椒粉，米酒，猪油，葵花油

做　　法：1. 取出鳗鱼的内脏，用热水烫去鳗鱼的表皮。

2. 洗净鳗鱼用菜刀切成块状，在一平盘内放成圈状。
3. 准备调料、锅内加入 1 茶匙盐、1/2 茶匙糖、1/2 茶匙白胡椒粉、1 茶匙米酒、一点猪油然后搅拌均匀，淋入鳗鱼块。
4. 盖上保鲜膜放入蒸锅，用大火蒸 7 分钟，然后关火，不要掀盖焖几分钟。
5. 除去保鲜膜，撒入葱粒和姜末，然后淋上烧热的葵花油。

# 41. Prawn with scrambled egg

Preparation time 7 minutes + Cooking time 2 minutes
Ingredients:      300g prawns, 2 eggs
                  sunflower oil, sesame seeds, salt

Method:

1. Shelled prawns and de-veined.
2. Fry the prawns in oil in a medium hot wok for 1 minute then set aside.
3. Beat the eggs together and add a pinch of salt.
4. Scramble the eggs in a hot wok for 30 seconds and adding the prawns fry for a further 30 seconds.
5. Sprinkle cooked sesame seeds and serve.

The prawns have sweet flavors that are well complimented by scrambled egg.

## 虾仁炒蛋

准备时间7分钟＋烹饪时间2分钟

材　　料：300克虾，2个鸡蛋，葵花油，芝麻，盐

做　　法：1. 虾去壳，去除背部黑线。
　　　　　2. 用中火炒虾仁1分钟，放置一边。
　　　　　3. 搅拌鸡蛋，加入一撮盐。
　　　　　4. 鸡蛋在锅内炒30秒，然后加入虾仁再炒30秒。
　　　　　5. 撒上煮熟的芝麻即可。

# 42. Sweat and sour fish fillet

Preparation time 25 minutes + Cooking time 15 minutes

Ingredients:　400g fish fillet

chilli bean sauce, ginger, salt, sugar, chilli pepper, rice wine, vinegar, soy sauce, garlic, starch, egg white, sunflower oil

Method:

1. Marinate the fish fillet with 2 pieces of ginger, 1/2 teaspoon wine, 1/2 teaspoon salt, 1 egg white 15 minutes.
2. Move the fish onto a dry plate and pat a little starch on fish fillet both side.
3. Heat the oil in a pan, add the fish fillet and use a medium heat to fry until both sides becomes brown and crispy then set aside.
4. Add a little more oil to the pan, the shredded spring onions and garlic, 1 teaspoon chilli bean sauce, 1 teaspoon wine and diced red chilli, 1 teaspoon vinegar, 1 teaspoon soy sauce and heat until simmering. Add the fish fillet stir-fry 30 seconds.

This is a traditional favourite and the sweet and sour recipe is world renowned.

## 糖醋鱼块

准备时间 25 分钟 + 烹饪时间 15 分钟

材　　料：400 克鱼块，辣豆瓣酱，姜片，盐，糖，辣椒，米酒，醋，酱油，蒜头，淀粉，蛋清，葵花油

做　　法：1. 把鱼块和 2 片姜、1/2 茶匙酒、1/2 茶匙盐、1 个蛋清一起腌 15 分钟。
2. 把鱼块放入一干燥的盘内，两面拍上淀粉。
3. 用一个平底锅热油，加入鱼块。用中火煎至两面变成金黄色且香脆。
4. 锅内再放入一点油、切碎的辣椒、放入葱粒和蒜末、1 茶匙辣豆瓣酱、1 茶匙酒、1 茶匙醋、1 茶匙酱油。加热直至煮沸。再加入鱼块另煮 30 秒即可。

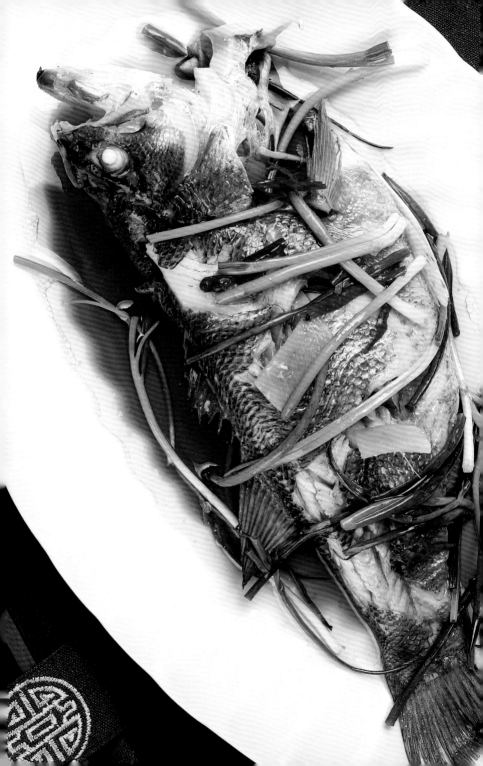

# 43. Steamed sea bass

Preparation time 10 minutes + Cooking time 8 minutes

Ingredients:     1 sea bass (any whole flat fish)

salt, spring onion, sunflower oil, fish sauce, soy sauce, ginger

Method:

1. Gut and wash the fish thoroughly.
2. Slash 2 slits in each side of the fish and place ginger in the slits, head and the body of the fish.
3. Rub a little salt onto the skin and rest on a flat plate for few minutes.
4. Steam the fish in a closed wok for 7-8 minutes.
5. Make a dressing from 1 tablespoon of oil, 2 tablespoons of soy sauce and 1 tablespoon of fish sauce and microwave for 30 seconds.
6. Take the steamed fish and sprinkle on sliced spring onions.
7. Pour the hot sauce over the fish and serve immediately.

By steaming the sea bass, the fish remains succulent and does not lose any of its flavors.

## 蒸 鱼

准备时间 10 分钟 + 烹饪时间 8 分钟

材     料：1 条鲈鱼(或整条扁平的鱼)，盐，青葱，葵花油，鱼露，酱油，姜片

做     法：1. 取出鱼的内脏，洗净。
2. 在鱼的两面各划 2 刀，塞入姜片，鱼的头部和内部也同样塞入姜片。
3. 抹少许盐在鱼的表面，等上几分钟。
4. 把鱼放入锅内用大火蒸 7~8 分钟。
5. 制作调料：1 汤匙油、2 汤匙酱油、1 汤匙鱼露用微波炉加热 30 秒。
6. 把鱼取出撒上葱段。
7. 淋上调料即食。

# 44. Prawns with cashew nuts

Preparation time 5 minutes + Cooking time 6 minutes

Ingredients: 300g prawns, 80g cashew nuts

rice wine, sunflower oil, salt

Method:

1. Wash peel and de-vein the prawns.
2. Heat the oil in a wok and brown the nuts then set aside.
3. Warm a little more oil in the wok and fry the prawns with a pinch of salt and a splash of rice wine for 1 minute until the colour of the prawns comes through, then add the nuts and fry for a further second.

The cashew nuts contain unsaturated fatty acids, calcium, iron, phosphor, zinc. It's a great brain food! The mixture of nut and prawn is extremely healthy and the smell of the prawns and nuts cooking together really whets your appetite.

## 腰果虾仁

准备时间 5 分钟 + 烹饪时间 6 分钟

材　　料：300 克虾，80 克腰果，米酒，葵花油，盐

做　　法：1. 把虾洗净去壳，用刀去除背部的黑线。

2. 锅内热油后，把腰果炒热至颜色变深，放在一边备用。

3. 锅内再放点油，等微热后放入虾仁后再放点酒和盐，炒 1 分钟左右，等颜色变深后加入腰果，再炒几秒钟。

# 45. Scallops with asparagus

Preparation time 15 minutes + Cooking time 3 minutes
Ingredients:　　6 shelled scallops, 1 bunch asparagus
　　　　　　　　rice wine, sesame seeds, groundnut oil, salt

Method:

1. Fry the sesame seeds until golden brown then place in a small bowl.
2. Lightly scour the scallops and cut the surface with light slash and steam until the colour turns opaque.
3. Peel the asparagus and cut off the harder ends then slice into long triangles and keep the tops.
4. Heat the oil until hot and fry the seasoned asparagus and scallops for 2 minutes and add 1/2 teaspoon salt and stir-fry 1 minutes.
5. Remove from the heat and mix the sesame seeds.

The combination of seafood and vegetable goes very well. The crunchiness of the asparagus offsets the delicate scallops.

## 鲜贝芦笋

准备时间 15 分钟 + 烹饪时间 3 分钟
材　　料：6 个鲜贝，1 束芦笋，米酒，芝麻，花生油，盐

做　　法：1. 把芝麻炒熟后放入一小碗内。
　　　　　2. 轻轻地冲洗鲜贝，表面轻划几刀，放入蒸锅蒸熟。
　　　　　3. 芦笋去皮并切除根部，再切成三角状，保留前端尖部。
　　　　　4. 锅内热油，放入芦笋和鲜贝炒 2 分钟，加 1/2 茶匙盐后再炒 1 分钟。
　　　　　5. 关火，盛盘后撒上熟芝麻。

# 46. Steamed crab

Preparation time 6 minutes + Cooking time 10 minutes

Ingredients:     1 large whole crab

rice vinegar, ginger

Method:

1. Wash the crab thoroughly with a brush and tie securely to a metal (wooden) frame.
2. Heat water in a covered wok, and using the frame to keep the crab out the water, steam for 10 minutes, move onto a big tray.
3. Carefully separate the shell of the limbs at every intervals using a cleaver or hammer. The hammer works best on the larger pinchers.
4. Remove and discard the yellow and white contents of the small stomach.
5. Serve with a pair of nut crackers and the vinegar mix the dice ginger to dip.

This is a high protein and microelement. A real delicacy in China, this dish is both full of flavour and nutritious.

## 蒸 蟹

准备时间6分钟+烹饪时间10分钟

材　　料：1只螃蟹，米醋和姜

做　　法：1. 用刷子把螃蟹洗净，绑在一个牢固的金属（木制）的支架上。

2. 锅内热水，放入螃蟹，蒸10分钟，放入一个大盘中。

3. 小心地分开蟹肚和蟹壳，大的蟹钳可以用小锤和菜刀敲碎。

4. 去除蟹内的腮和白色小胃。

5. 准备一把果仁夹子和一小碟醋混合姜丝。

# 47. Seafood bowl

Preparation time 30 minutes + Cooking time 15 minutes

Ingredients:　　celery, carrot, asparagus, mushroom, squid, prawn, fish
steak, scallop (random number)
ginger, rice wine, spring onion, salt, chicken soup (chicken
stock), wild pepper, groundnut oil, white pepper powder

Method:

1. Wash and slice all the vegetables, separate the scallops, dice the squid
and fish steak.

2. Heat the oil in a wok to medium temperature, put all seafood add 3 pieces
of ginger, a bit of wild pepper, 1 tablespoon salt and 1 tablespoon wine stir-
fry for 3 minutes.

3. Move to a big ceramic pot, add all the vegetables and 200g chicken soup
(1 cube chicken stock in a cup of water). Cooking with low heat, stew for 10
minutes with the lid on.

4. Turn off the fire, drizzle a little white pepper powder and garnish with shredded spring onions then prepare to serve.

💡 Highly prized along the coast of South China, seafood is one of the most
expensive and sought-after dishes.

## 海鲜锅

准备时间 30 分钟 + 烹饪时间 15 分钟

材　　料：芹菜，胡萝卜，芦笋，蘑菇，鱿鱼，虾，鱼块，鲜贝（数量随意），生姜，米酒，青
葱，盐，鸡汤（鸡精块），花椒，花生油，白胡椒粉

做　　法：1. 洗净切片所有的蔬菜。鲜贝切成两半，鱼块及鱿鱼切块。
2. 锅内热油到适中的温度。放入所有的海鲜和 3 片姜、1 汤匙盐、1 汤匙米酒、少
许花椒，翻炒 3 分钟。
3. 移入大煲内，放入所有的蔬菜和海鲜，倒入 200 克的鸡汤（一块鸡精块兑一杯水）。
盖上盖用小火炖 10 分钟。
4. 关火，撒入一些白胡椒粉和葱粒即可。

# 48. Smoked fish

Preparation time 5 minutes + Cooking time 20 minutes

Ingredients:      400g fish fillet

spring onion, soy sauce, ginger, Chinese five spice powder, rice wine, sugar, red chilli

Method:

1. Make a marinade from 5 tablespoons of soy sauce, 1 teaspoon five spice powder, 1 tablespoon of rice wine, 3 pieces of ginger, 3 sliced spring onions, 1 tablespoons of sugar and 1 sliced red chilli.

2. Heat the oil in a wok, then hot fry the fish until both sides are golden brown.

3. Place the fish in the marinade sauce, marinate for 10 minutes then drain and serve.

This is very tasty either hot or cold and can be kept up to 3 days after preparation.

## 熏 鱼

准备时间 5 分钟 + 烹饪时间 20 分钟

材　　料：400 克鱼片，青葱，酱油，姜片，五香粉，米酒，糖，红辣椒

做　　法：1. 做一个腌料：用 5 汤匙酱油、1 茶匙五香粉、1 汤匙米酒、3 片姜、3 根青葱、1 汤匙糖和 1 个切碎的红辣椒。

2. 锅内热油，煎鱼直到两面都呈金黄色。

3. 把鱼放入腌料中，腌 10 分钟再沥干即可。

# 49. Chinese leaves with fish balls

Preparation time 5 minutes + Cooking time 4 minutes
Ingredients:      1/2 head of Chinese leaves, 3 fish balls
                  vegetable oil, salt, vegetable stock (optional)

Method:

1. Roughly chop several Chinese leaves and split fish balls.
2. Heat the oil in a wok under a medium heat then add the leaves and fish balls quick fry for 1 minute and a pinch of salt to fry for 3 minutes.
3. Mix 2 tablespoons of hot water with the 1/2 teaspoon vegetable stock and pour into the wok.
4. Fry for one more minute with the lid on.

A fantastically fresh tasting dish, the meaty fish balls compliment the savoury Chinese leaves very well.

## 白菜鱼丸

准备时间 5 分钟 + 烹饪时间 4 分钟

材　　料：半棵白菜，3 个鱼丸，蔬菜油，盐，蔬菜精（选用）

做　　法：1. 把白菜切成几段，把鱼丸切开。
　　　　　2. 锅内热油到 7 成热，放入白菜和鱼丸，快速翻炒 1 分钟，加入少量的盐再炒 3 分钟。
　　　　　3. 放入 2 汤匙水和 1/2 茶匙蔬菜精（选用）。
　　　　　4. 盖上锅盖焖 1 分钟即可。

Rice Nood Desert

米饭、面食、甜品

# 50. Chow mein

Preparation time 8 minutes + Cooking time 7 minutes

Ingredients:  200g thick noodles, 2 bok choy (or any green coloured vegetable) cloves garlic, vegetable oil, salt, barbecue sauce, light soy sauce

Method:

1. Cook the noodles in a pan of boiling water for 3-5 minutes, then drain and put them in cold  water for 2 minutes, drain thoroughly.
2. Cut the bok choy into 3 parts.
3. Heat oil in the wok and fry the shredded garlic until light brown.
4. Add the noodles, bok choy, 1/2 tablespoon of barbeque sauce, a pinch of salt and 1 tablespoon light soy sauce to dress.
5. Stir-fry on a high heat for 2 minutes, then use lower heat fry for a further 3 minutes.

This classic recipe is done in the old fashioned way.

## 炒 面

准备时间8分钟 + 烹饪时间7分钟

材　料：200克面条，2棵青菜（或其他绿叶菜），蒜头，蔬菜油，盐，烧烤酱，生抽酱油

做　法：1. 在沸水中放入面条，煮3~5分钟后沥干，放入冷水中2分钟，再彻底沥干。
2. 把青菜切成3段。
3. 锅内热油后放入蒜末，快炒一下直到颜色变深。
4. 加入面条、青菜、1/2汤匙烧烤酱、少许盐、1汤匙生抽酱油。
5. 用大火翻炒2分钟后，再用小火翻炒3分钟。

# 51. Wontons

Preparation time 20 minutes + Cooking time 10 minutes

Ingredients: 20 wonton peels, 4 bok choy, 150g pork mince
spring onion, egg white, chicken stock, rice wine, sunflower oil, salt

Method:

1. Boil the bok choy in water for 6 minutes, and then drain and finely chopped (can use a food processor).
2. Mix the pork mince with 1 egg white, a little salt, 1/3 teaspoon wine, 1 teaspoon sesame oil and blend with the shredded bok choy.
3. Wrap the balls in the wonton cases, two edges seal with a dab of water put to a tray.
4. Bring the water to the boil and then add the wonton when wonton begin to float, add 1/2 a cup of water to cool down then bring to the boil again.
5. Boil a separate pot of water make a soup, 1 chicken stock cube, 1 teaspoon of sunflower oil, shredded spring onions and 1/3 teaspoon of salt.
6. When the wontons are finished, drain and add to the soup.

💡 This is a classic dish and very easy to prepare. It can be looked on as a snack (Dim Sum) or main course.

## 馄 饨

准备时间 20 分钟 + 烹饪时间 10 分钟

材　料：20 张馄饨皮，4 棵青菜，150 克猪肉糜，青葱，蛋清，鸡精，米酒，葵花油，盐

做　法：1. 把青菜煮 6 分钟，然后沥干切碎(可以用食品加工机)。
2. 用一个蛋清、一撮盐、1/3 茶匙酒、1 茶匙芝麻油和青菜肉糜搅拌。
3. 馄饨皮两边沾水，放入馅后对折，把两头捏牢即可。
4. 把馄饨放入沸水，待漂浮上来后倒入 1/2 杯水，再焖煮直至再次沸腾为止。
5. 另外做一汤料，把 1 块鸡精、1 茶匙葵花油、切碎的青葱和 1/3 茶匙盐放入汤水中煮沸。
6. 当馄饨煮熟后，沥干放入汤碗中即可。

# 52. Egg pancake

Preparation time 5 minutes + Cooking time 4 minutes

Ingredients:    1 egg, plain flour
spring onion, mashed potato (optional), sunflower oil, salt

Method:

1. Using a large bowl mix a dough from 4 tablespoons of flour and twice as much water and 1/4 teaspoon salt.
2. Slice the spring onions.
3. Use a hot frying pan and pour in oil cover the pan and pour in the dough mixture.
4. Break an egg evenly cover the pancake and add some spring onions (and mashed potato) until the egg begins to set.
5. Turn the pancake over to fry on the other side for 1 minute move into a plate and serve hot.

The egg pancake suits breakfast and afternoon tea. The flavor can be altered by changing the amount of sugar or salt used.

## 蛋 饼

准备时间 5 分钟 + 烹饪时间 4 分钟

材　　料：1 个鸡蛋，面粉，葱，土豆泥（选用），葵花油，盐

做　　法：1. 用一个大碗放入 4 汤匙面粉和两倍的水和 1/4 茶匙盐，搅拌成面糊。
　　　　　2. 把青葱切碎。
　　　　　3. 用平底锅倒入油加热，倒入面糊。
　　　　　4. 敲开鸡蛋均匀地涂在饼上，撒上青葱（土豆泥）直到鸡蛋变熟。
　　　　　5. 翻转另一面再煎 1 分钟即可。

# 53. Salmon fish rice

Preparation time 5 minutes + Cooking time 7 minutes

Ingredients:    2 steaks Salmon filets no skin (cod), 1 bowl cooked rice
butter, salt, soy sauce, sesame seed, lime

Method:

1. Sprinkle soy sauce on both sides of the salmon and marinate for 5 minutes.
2. Melt the 60g butter in a hot pan and add the salmon and pinch of salt to fry both sides until brown.
3. Use a fork to separate the fish and blend with cooked rice. Add 1 teaspoon soy sauce and drizzle cooked sesame seeds, sprinkle over the lime juice.

So quick and healthy, the aroma and taste of the salmon encourages any appetite.

## 三文鱼拌饭

准备时间5分钟 + 烹饪时间7分钟

材    料：2块三文鱼不带皮（鳕鱼），1碗米饭，黄油，盐，酱油，芝麻，青柠

做法：1. 三文鱼两面撒上酱油腌5分钟。
2. 把60克黄油溶解在平底热锅中，放入三文鱼和一小撮盐两面煎熟。
3. 用叉子分开三文鱼与饭一起搅拌，加入1茶匙酱油、烧熟的芝麻，撒入几滴青柠汁即可。

# 54. Spring rolls

Preparation time 30 minutes + Cooking time 10 minutes

Ingredients: 1/2 head of Chinese leaves, 300g pork mince, 20-25 spring roll wrappers

salt, rice wine, sunflower oil, starch, rice vinegar

Method:

1. Dice the Chinese leaves into the thin long strips.
2. Using a small bowl add 2 teaspoons starch flour and pour in 80g water so that the water become opaque.
3. Heat the oil in a wok. First add the pork mince to quick fry with 1/2 teaspoon rice wine then add the Chinese leaves to stir-fry for 4 minutes. Add 1/2 tablespoon salt and starch water and fry for a further minute until the mixture sticks together.
4. Move the Chinese leaves onto a big tray and wait for the temperature to cool down.
5. Separate the spring roll wrapper. Fold every wrapper with 1 tablespoon of Chinese leaves and mince to wrap into a spring roll, seal it's edge with a mixture of starch and water.
6. Heat the oil in a pan until 70% hot, turn down the heat to medium heat and add the spring roll to fry both sides until golden brown.
7. Drain the oil from the spring rolls then move onto a plate. Serve hot and with rice vinegar.

Simple to make, and flexible to your own tastes, these are brilliant snack.

## 春 卷

准备时间30分钟+烹饪时间10分钟

材　　料：半棵白菜，300克猪肉糜，20~25张春卷皮，盐，米酒，葵花油，淀粉，米醋

做　　法：1. 把白菜切成细长条。
　　　　　2. 在小碗内放入2茶匙淀粉、80克水搅拌，使水变成不透明状。
　　　　　3. 锅内热油，先放入猪肉糜快炒，放入1/2茶匙米酒，再加入白菜翻炒4分钟。加入1/2汤匙盐和水淀粉。再略炒片刻直到黏稠。
　　　　　4. 把馅料放入一个大盘冷却。
　　　　　5. 分开春卷皮，每张皮内放入1汤匙馅。卷成桶状，边缘部分用水和淀粉的混合液封紧。
　　　　　6. 油加温到7成热，用中火煎春卷直至颜色变金黄色。
　　　　　7. 春卷沥干油，放置盘内，蘸米醋食用。

# 55. Bok choy rice

Preparation time 15 minutes + Cooking time 45 minutes

Ingredients:　　3 bok choy, 80g bacon, 400g rice

salt, pork fat, sunflower oil

Method:

1. Use a pot or electric cooking pot to cook the rice, 400g rice needs 600g water.
2. Boil the rice until the majority of the water has evaporated and the rice cooked half-way.
3. Wash the bok choy and bacon and chop into tiny pieces.
4. Heat the oil in a wok, add the bok choy and bacon with 1 teaspoon salt to quick fry for 1 minute.
5. Move the bok choy and bacon to the rice pot, add 1 teaspoon pork fat and mix well.
6. Cover with a lid and cook until the rice done.

💡 **A vegetable dish that is high in nutrients.**

# 菜 饭

准备时间 15 分钟 + 烹饪时间 45 分钟

材　　料：3 棵青菜，80 克咸肉，400 克米，盐，猪油，葵花油

做法：1. 用一个锅或电饭煲煮饭。400 克米饭需要加 600 克水。

2. 煮饭直至半熟状态。
3. 洗净青菜，咸肉切成小片。
4. 锅内热油，然后放入青菜和咸肉，加 1 茶匙盐快炒 1 分钟。
5. 把青菜和咸肉放入饭锅，加入 1 茶匙猪油拌匀。
6. 盖上锅盖直到米饭煮熟。

# 56. Pumpkin Cake

Preparation time 30 minutes + Cooking time 8 minutes

Ingredients:     300g pumpkin, 100g plain flour
                 sesame seeds, honey, water (milk), sunflower oil

Method:

1. Peel the pumpkin, take out the seeds and chop into big chunks.
2. Move pumpkin into a steamer to steam until soft. Use the back of a spoon and squash the pumpkin then add 2 teaspoons honey, 100g plain flour, a bit of water or milk and blend well.
3. Use hands to form into round cake shapes and dip the sesame seeds into the surface.
4. Heat the oil in a pan on a medium heat then add the pumpkin cakes to fry until brown.

There are very few traditional dishes that can be called vegetarian. But this is one of the best.

## 南瓜饼

准备时间 30 分钟 + 烹饪时间 8 分钟

材　　料：300 克南瓜，100 克面粉，芝麻，蜂蜜，水（牛奶），葵花油

做　　法：1. 南瓜去皮，拿掉里面的籽，切成大块。
　　　　　2. 把南瓜放入锅内煮直至变软，拿出用汤匙背面把南瓜压成泥状，加入 2 茶匙蜂蜜、100 克面粉，用水或牛奶搅拌均匀。
　　　　　3. 压成饼状，表面撒上芝麻粒。
　　　　　4. 锅内热油，用中火煎直至颜色金黄。

# 57. Egg Fried Rice

Preparation time 5 minutes + Cooking time 5 minutes

Ingredients: 2 eggs, 1 bowl of cooked rice, 1 Chinese sausage. sweet corn or shrimp (optional), peas
spring onion, salt, sunflower oil

Method:

1. Beat the eggs in a bowl and add a little salt blend well.
2. Pour oil in a pan and add sliced sausage to fry for 1 minute then remove.
3. Reheat the pan with some more oil, pour in the egg and use a fork or chopstick to whisk. Add the rice, sausage, sweet corn and a little salt and fry for 3 minutes.
4. Turn down the heat and sprinkle some shredded spring onions to cook for a further minute.

💡 You can use shrimp and peas in place of sausage with sweet corn depending on your taste. This is a popular dish for lunch, dinner or as a snack.

## 蛋炒饭

准备时间 5 分钟 + 烹饪时间 5 分钟

材　料：2 个鸡蛋，1 碗饭，1 根香肠，玉米粒或虾仁（选用），青豆，青葱，盐，葵花油

做　法：1. 鸡蛋放在碗里，加入一点盐，搅拌均匀。
2. 锅内热油，加入已经切片的香肠，炒 1 分种，盛出备用。
3. 锅内热油，倒入鸡蛋并用叉子或筷子快速搅拌，加入饭、香肠、玉米粒、一点盐，翻炒 3 分钟。
4. 调制小火，撒上葱粒，翻炒几分钟即可。

# 58. Traditional porridge

Preparation time 2 minutes + Cooking time 30-40 minutes
Ingredients:     100g rice
water, sunflower oil

Method:

1. Take 100g rice and add 500g of hot water and heat until boiling.
2. Turn down the heat and stew for 20 minutes with lid on, sprinkle 3 drops of oil and use a chop stick to mix several times until a little sticky.
3. If you want some more combinations you can add chicken meat, pork, vegetable or seafood and cook together for 10 minutes.

Porridge is good food for old people or babies and is full of slow burning carbohydrates.

## 粥

准备时间2分钟 + 烹饪时间30~40分钟
材　　料：100克米，水，葵花油

做　　法：1. 100克的米加入500克的水加热直至煮沸。
2. 盖上锅盖，再煮20分钟，然后打开锅盖撒上3滴油，用筷子搅拌直到有稠密感。
3. 如果想味道更鲜美可加入其他材料，如鸡肉、猪肉、蔬菜或海鲜，加上以上材料后再煮10分钟。

# 59. Mango Pudding

Preparation time 40 minutes + Cooking time 10 minutes

Ingredients:　　mango jam, thick cream

milk, sugar, gelatine

Method:

1. Put the mango jam in a pan and heat until cooked then turn off the fire.
2. Add the several spoons of cream and sugar depend on your taste.
3. Pour in milk and blend well then turn on the heat again, sprinkle in the powdered gelatine and meanwhile use a stick to mix well.
4. When the mixture begins to bubble turn off the heat and pour the mixture into several flower shape metal or ceramic ramekins.
5. Cover with cling film and put in the refrigerator until set.

Extraordinary, but extremely well received by anyone with a sweet tooth!

## 芒果布丁

准备时间 40 分钟＋烹饪时间 10 分钟

材　　料：芒果酱，奶油，牛奶，糖，白明胶

做　　法：1. 在一个锅内倒入芒果酱加热直至烧热，熄火。

2. 撒入几匙奶油和糖，根据自己的口味选量。

3. 放入牛奶搅拌，加热撒入粉状的白明胶，同时用筷子搅拌。

4. 当混合物开始起泡，关火把液体分别倒入几个花状的金属或陶瓷模具中。

5. 盖上保鲜膜放入冰箱直至冷却即可。

# 60. Papaya milk

Preparation time 5 minutes
Ingredients:　　　200g papaya, 1 cup of milk, vanilla ice cream

Method:
Take papaya cubes with milk and a few spoons of ice cream. Mix in a food processor for few a seconds. Pour into a large glass to serve.

Strongly recommend, this great fruit contains a variety of vitamins, especial vitamin C, which is 48 times higher than apples. This is a good drink for hot days or as a dessert.

## 木瓜牛奶

准备时间 5 分钟
材　　料：200 克木瓜，1 杯牛奶，香草冰激凌

做　　法：把木瓜果肉，牛奶和几匙香草冰激凌倒入食品加工机搅拌几秒即可，倒入玻璃杯中即可。

Index

索 引

# Index
索引

| 1.Cucumber salad | 凉拌黄瓜 | 10-11 |
| 2.White radish salad | 凉拌萝卜 | 12-13 |
| 3.Aubergine salad | 凉拌茄子 | 14-15 |
| 4.Potato salad | 土豆色拉 | 16-17 |
| 5.Ma-po tofu | 麻婆豆腐 | 18-19 |
| 6.Bok choy fry mushrooms | 青菜蘑菇 | 20-21 |
| 7.Tomato scrambled eggs | 番茄炒蛋 | 22-23 |
| 8.Green pepper fried potato | 青椒土豆丝 | 24-25 |
| 9.Stewed aubergine | 油焖茄子 | 26-27 |
| 10.Steamed egg pudding | 蒸 蛋 | 28-29 |
| 11.Spicy Chinese leaves | 辣白菜 | 30-31 |
| 12.Spinach soup | 菠菜汤 | 32-33 |
| 13.Vermicelli with fried tofu soup | 油豆腐粉丝汤 | 34-35 |
| 14.Celery with dried tofu and pork mince | 芹菜豆腐干肉丝 | 38-39 |
| 15.Pork kidneys with green chilli | 青椒腰花 | 40-41 |
| 16.Beef and radish stew | 萝卜牛腩 | 42-43 |
| 17.Roast duck legs | 烤鸭腿 | 44-45 |
| 18.Avocado with beef mince | 牛油果牛肉糜 | 46-47 |
| 19.Beef and potato curry | 咖喱土豆牛肉 | 48-49 |
| 20.Spring onion chicken | 葱油鸡 | 50-51 |
| 21.Beef stew tomatoes | 番茄炖牛肉 | 52-53 |
| 22.Hui guo pork | 回锅肉 | 54-55 |
| 23.Curried chicken legs | 咖喱鸡腿 | 56-57 |
| 24.Gong bao chicken | 宫爆鸡丁 | 58-59 |
| 25.Cha shao | 叉 烧 | 60-61 |
| 26.Easy microwave chicken wings | 微波炉鸡翅 | 62-63 |
| 27.Pork with eggs | 肉焖蛋 | 64-65 |
| 28.Sichuan kou shui chicken | 四川口水鸡 | 66-67 |
| 29.Pineapple beef | 菠萝牛肉 | 68-69 |
| 30.Cauliflower with pork | 花菜肉片 | 70-71 |
| 31.Cheese pork steak | 干酪猪排 | 72-73 |
| 32.Snap peas with Chinese sausage | 荷兰豆炒香肠 | 74-75 |

| | | |
|---|---|---|
| 33.Fried beef strips with celery | 芹菜牛肉丝 | 76-77 |
| 34.Big meat ball | 狮子头 | 78-79 |
| 35.Chicken fry bean sprouts | 银芽鸡丝 | 80-81 |
| 36.Bok choy meat ball soup | 青菜肉丸汤 | 82-83 |
| 37.Luo song soup | 罗宋汤 | 84-85 |
| 38.Hot pot | 火 锅 | 86-87 |
| 39.King prawn stew | 油爆虾 | 90-91 |
| 40.Steamed eel | 蒸鳗鱼 | 92-93 |
| 41.Prawn with scrambled egg | 虾仁炒蛋 | 94-95 |
| 42.Sweat and sour fish fillet | 糖醋鱼块 | 96-97 |
| 43.Steamed sea bass | 蒸 鱼 | 98-99 |
| 44.Prawns with cashew nuts | 腰果虾仁 | 100-101 |
| 45.Scallops with asparagus | 鲜贝芦笋 | 102-103 |
| 46.Steamed crab | 蒸 蟹 | 104-105 |
| 47.Seafood bowl | 海鲜锅 | 106-107 |
| 48.Smoked fish | 熏 鱼 | 108-109 |
| 49.Chinese leaves with fish balls | 白菜鱼丸 | 110-111 |
| 50.Chow mein | 炒 面 | 114-115 |
| 51.Wontons | 馄 饨 | 116-117 |
| 52.Egg pancake | 蛋 饼 | 118-119 |
| 53.Salmon fish rice | 三文鱼拌饭 | 120-121 |
| 54.Spring rolls | 春 卷 | 122-123 |
| 55.Bok choy rice | 菜 饭 | 124-125 |
| 56.Pumpkin Cake | 南瓜饼 | 126-127 |
| 57.Egg Fried Rice | 蛋炒饭 | 128-129 |
| 58.Traditional porridge | 粥 | 130-131 |
| 59.Mango Pudding | 芒果布丁 | 132-133 |
| 60.Papaya milk | 木瓜牛奶 | 134-135 |

图书在版编目 (CIP) 数据

中式家常菜 / 刘陆陆 编著. —上海：上海世界图书出版公司，2006. 10

ISBN 7-5062-8504-5

Ⅰ. 中...　Ⅱ. 刘...　Ⅲ. 菜谱－中国－汉、英　Ⅳ. TS972. 182

中国版本图书馆 CIP 数据核字(2006) 第 097503 号

# 中式家常菜

### 刘陆陆 编著

上海世界图书出版公司出版发行

上海市尚文路 185 号 B 楼

（公司电话：021-63783016 转发行科）

邮政编码 200010

上海精英彩色印务有限公司印刷

如有印刷装订质量问题，请与印刷厂联系

（质检科电话：021-56941616）

各地新华书店经销

开本：890 × 1240　1/32　印张：4.375　字数：80 000
2006 年 10 月第 1 版　2006 年 10 月第 1 次印刷
印数：1-3 000
ISBN 7-5062-8504-5/T · 134
定价：48.00 元
http://www.wpcsh.com.cn